Special Edward

Eric Walters

Orca currents

ORCA BOOK PUBLISHERS

Library and Archives Canada Cataloguing in Publication

Walters, Eric, 1957-
Special Edward / written by Eric Walters.

(Orca currents)
ISBN 978-1-55469-092-3 (pbk.).--ISBN 978-1-55469-096-1 (bound)

I. Title. II. Series: Orca currents

PS8595.A598S625 2009   jC813'.54   C2009-900016-4

Summary: In an attempt to gain lowered expectations and extra time for
tests, Edward fakes a special education designation.

First published in the United States, 2009
Library of Congress Control Number: 2008943735

Orca Book Publishers gratefully acknowledges the support for its publishing
programs provided by the following agencies: the Government of Canada
through the Book Publishing Industry Development Program and the
Canada Council for the Arts, and the Province of British Columbia
through the BC Arts Council and the Book Publishing Tax Credit.

Cover design by Teresa Bubela
Cover photography by Getty Images

Orca Book Publishers
PO Box 5626, Station B
Victoria, BC Canada
V8R 6S4

Orca Book Publishers
PO Box 468
Custer, WA USA
98240-0468

www.orcabook.com
Printed and bound in Canada.
Printed on 100% PCW recycled paper.

12 11 10 09 • 4 3 2 1

chapter one

Nervously I peeked into the class through the door's little window. Everybody had their heads down, writing a math test. If I had remembered we had a test, I would have worked harder to be on time. Actually, if I'd remembered there was a test, I would have studied. Okay, studied might be the wrong word, an exaggeration, but I would have at least done some review...probably...maybe. Okay, who was I trying to fool? There was at least a fifty-fifty chance

I would have blown off the studying even if I knew the test was coming.

I looked at my watch. The period had started twelve minutes ago. I was officially late, at least officially late for math. Some teachers would let ten or fifteen minutes slide. Mr. Mathews did not believe in letting anything slide. Typical.

Math teachers are always more sticky about being punctual than other teachers. Maybe because they work with numbers, they like to show off that they could tell time.

I could tell time, I just didn't feel any need to be controlled by it. I always thought that I owned the watch; the watch didn't own me.

My drama teacher, Ms. Collins, was much, much cooler about time. You could roll into her class halfway through and as long as you gave her what she called "a good lie," she didn't worry about it. I loved coming up with stories. Sometimes I was late on purpose so I could tell a story. It was pretty amazing that you could be late and get applause from your teacher.

I didn't expect Mr. Mathews to cheer, and the longer I stood here, the later I was getting.

I pushed open the door and slipped in. Almost everybody looked up at me. Quiet wasn't quiet enough in a room where you could hear a pin drop.

"Edward," Mr. Mathews said sternly, "you're late."

"Are you sure, sir? I was thinking that maybe all of you were just early."

A couple of people laughed. Mr. Mathews wasn't one of them.

"Do you have a late slip?" he asked.

"Sorry, no, I didn't think I was that late."

"You are and you need one."

"Can I get one after?" I asked. "By the time I get down to the office and back, I'll have even less time to do the test. I think I really need all the time I can get."

"That logic is hard to argue with."

"So I can go later?"

He held out a test.

I took the test and shuffled over to the empty desk in the back corner—my usual spot beside my friend Cody. He glanced up and gave me a little nod as I settled into my seat.

I started to look at the test. The first page was all algebra—the show-your-work sort that I hated. Wasn't it hard enough to get the right answer without having to show how you did it? It eliminated the element of luck, and I depended heavily on that element.

I flipped to the second page. It was all multiple-choice questions. I loved multiple-choice. Usually one or two of the answers were obviously wrong. That meant that there was often a fifty-percent chance of success, and fifty percent was the mark I aimed for.

I turned to the third page. Word problems. That was just plain mean. This was math not English. If it was English, at least I'd have a chance to bluff my way through it. In math there was no bluff, no bull, just right and wrong—and wrong was most often the winning side.

Well, there was no point in complaining. I had to get started. I dug into my bag and rummaged around for a pencil. I searched the different compartments. No pencil. No pen. Not even a crayon. I looked around the room.

Sitting on the other side of Cody was Simon. He had a pencil that he was using to write the test. There were two others on the corner of his desk, along with a ruler and a perfect never-been-used eraser. I guess Simon never made a mistake, and he didn't need to use his eraser. Simon was smart but not annoying about it. He was okay.

I stuck up my hand. "Mr. Mathews, I don't seem to have a pencil."

He let out a big sigh. "Why am I not surprised, Edward?"

Mr. Mathews was one of the only people in the world to call me Edward, him and one of my great-aunts. And my mother when she was mad at me—Edward Philip Wilson, she'd say. That was a guarantee I was in trouble. Whenever she called me that, I just started apologizing. It was faster and easier. Everybody else in the world just called me Ed, or Eddy, or by my nickname, Fast Eddy.

I'd gotten that handle in grade six. It wasn't that I was that fast a runner, but I was pretty fast at running off my mouth— Fast Eddy. I could talk myself out of any trouble. Of course, most of the time talking got me into the trouble to begin with. Most people thought and then spoke. With me the words just came out so fast that it was like I heard them before I'd even thought about them.

"Simon has extra pencils...can I borrow a pencil?"

Simon startled and looked at me. Before he could answer, I got up and grabbed one of his pencils.

"Thanks, I appreciate it," I said.

What I also appreciated was how clearly he printed and how, in a quick glance, I had the answers to the last two questions on page one. Way to go, Simon. Way to go, Fast Eddy.

chapter two

The bell sounded, and I jumped in my seat. I'd been so lost in thought that I hadn't noticed the end of the period sneaking up on me. Where had the last fifty minutes gone?

All around me kids started to gather their things. There was a lot of happy noise—talking, laughing and joking—as they moved to the door.

I looked down at my test. I was still only three-quarters of the way through the third page. I'd left a couple of multiple-choices and at least two questions on the first page. My plan was to go back and look at them again once I'd finished. That was always my plan, although there were lots of tests I never quite finished.

Kids dropped their tests on Mr. Mathews's desk on their way out. On a non-test day, I was one of the first out the door. Sometimes I could find myself in the hall when the sound of the bell was still echoing off the walls.

Not today. I needed to keep going. I was sure I was close to a passing grade, but I might need another mark or two. I'd managed to pass all my courses in grade nine, and so far grade ten was working out the same. Of course, when I said pass, that's just about what I did—I was a solid fifty-five-percent average.

My parents and my teachers were always on me about "pulling up my socks" and "putting my nose to the grindstone" and how I had to "buckle down and get to work." I wasn't sure how my socks, a buckle or a grindstone—whatever the heck that was—would help me get better marks, and I wasn't going to find out.

My parents always lectured that I was too smart to be just scraping by. I was smart enough to know that a fifty-five gave you the same credit as a ninety-five.

I knew if I worked harder I could get a higher grade, but so far nobody had given me a convincing enough argument that it was worth the extra work. Besides, a ninety-five was definitely out of the question. If I ever got a ninety-five I think they'd test me for steroids. No, steroids would only help me run away from work faster...maybe that would have helped today.

Some people thought that school only involved learning and tests. What a bizarre thought. A big chunk of school was social. I was exceptionally good at that part. They just didn't give out marks for it.

Everybody liked me. Well, everybody except for a few of the teachers. Sometimes they took it personally when you didn't do well in their subjects. It was as if not liking history meant you didn't like them. That was stupid. I guess it also didn't help that some teachers didn't really have what you'd call a sense of humor—or at least my humor. Things that I thought were hilarious they didn't get, and they thought I was laughing at them. Okay, sometimes I *was* laughing at them, but not always. Most of the time I was just joking around.

I did exactly what I needed to get by in school. I wasn't about to give up on friends, sports, video games, going out, girls—well, the hope of girls—the Internet, TV, music and a hundred other things. I was surprised I had time to get a fifty-five.

I put my head down and tried to focus on the question I'd been working on. The answer had been startled out of my head by the bell. I looked at it again and miraculously the answer came back. I scribbled it down. It looked right.

I flipped back to the first page. I didn't have time to put down all the work, but I thought I knew the answer to one of the questions. I had no idea how I came to the answer, but I was pretty sure it was right. I wouldn't get all the marks but I'd still get partial marks. I wrote down the answer.

It started to get quiet again as the room emptied. I just needed another two or three minutes to get through the multiple-choice questions.

"Edward," Mr. Mathews said.

I didn't have time for a conversation. If I ignored him, maybe he'd go away and I could do a couple more questions.

"Edward!" he said louder. "Time is up."

"I'm almost finished."

I kept my head down and kept working. I ticked off the first missed question and—

"I need your paper, right now." He loomed over me.

"I have lunch next. Couldn't I just have a few more minutes?" I asked.

"Sorry," he said. "Rules are rules. You're only allowed the allotted time for the test."

"But I came in late," I argued.

"That is a mistake you probably shouldn't make again. Time is up." He stuck out his hand.

I wanted to argue, but I knew there was no point. I went to hand him the paper and then pulled it back. I quickly ticked answers to the two multiple-choice questions that I hadn't answered. That was probably worth one mark—two, if I was lucky—although I wasn't feeling that lucky.

I gave him my test. "Well, I came close to finishing."

"I don't think you've ever finished one of my tests," he said.

"Obviously you make them too long or else I could finish them," I joked, trying to coax a smile out of him.

He didn't laugh. That man had no sense of humor.

I gathered up my things and started for the door when my eye was caught by motion. There, sitting in the other back corner, was Zach, still working on his test. I skidded to a stop.

"Excuse me," I said to Mr. Mathews.

"Yes?"

I pointed at Zach.

"Zach is not your concern."

"But why is he still writing the test?"

"As I said, that's not your concern."

"Well...actually it is," I said. "If he can still be writing, then I can still be writing."

"Good-bye, Edward. Go to lunch."

"I'm not hungry. Just let me finish up the test. Five more minutes and—"

"Out...now," he ordered.

"But—"

"No buts." He walked over to the door and motioned for me to leave.

"This isn't fair," I said as I passed.

"This is very fair. Go."

This was a first. I'd been tossed out of a class before, but never tossed after a class was over and when I wanted to stay.

I mumbled under my breath—loud enough for him to hear, but not loud enough for him to hear exactly what I was saying.

I stepped outside, and to my shock he stepped out into the hall as well and closed the door. Maybe he had heard some of my mumblings.

"This situation is like an oxymoron," he said.

"Who are you calling a moron?" I snapped.

"Not a moron, an oxymoron."

"That sounds like a stupid oxen."

He laughed. Now that was a shock. Maybe bad jokes were the key.

"It means two things that don't go together," Mr. Mathews said. "Like you and wanting to stay after class. Those are two things that aren't usually contained in the same thought."

"Okay, I guess that makes sense."

"I wanted to explain why Zach is allowed more time than you."

"Yeah, I'd like to hear that," I agreed. Had Zach slipped him a couple of bucks, brought him a coffee, what? I'd be willing to do those things.

"Zach is designated as requiring additional support," Mr. Mathews said.

Now we were back to me not understanding. What did he mean by *additional support?* Did that mean he had inserts in his shoes or special socks or one of those cushiony pads for his chair?

"Zach is exceptional," Mr. Mathews said.

Zach didn't seem that exceptional to me. There was a girl in our class—Elizabeth—who was truly exceptional...exceptionally fine. But Zach just seemed like one of the guys.

"And because of his exceptionality, he gets extra time to complete tests."

"Hold on," I said. "So what exactly is it about Zach that makes him exceptional?"

"I'm not really sure," Mr. Mathews said with a shrug. "I just know that he has a designation of exceptionality, which means he requires special services."

This was all starting to make sense. "So you're saying that Zach is special ed."

"He is designated exceptional," he repeated. "Exactly."

"And he gets extra time, and I don't because I'm not exceptional."

"Yes, he receives extra time, among other things, as support," Mr. Mathews said.

"What sort of other things could happen?"

"Some designated students get to use

spell-checkers, or laptop computers or they have scribes to assist with tests."

"What's a scribe?"

"Somebody who writes the test for them."

My eyes widened in shock. "You mean they can get somebody really smart to write the test for them? They don't even have to take the test?"

"No, no!" Mr. Mathews exclaimed. "They still have to take the test, but somebody else does the actual writing. The scribe writes what they're told to write."

"Okay, that's not quite as good, but it's still pretty good. So who do I see about getting this done for me, this exceptional stuff?"

"Well, you don't really see anybody. It has to do with testing," Mr. Mathews said.

"Testing? But I don't want to take another test. I'm having enough trouble with the tests I'm taking already."

"Look, I'm not the best person to talk to about this. Go see your guidance counselor. I'm sure she can explain it to you."

"Thanks. I'll do that."

I strolled down the hall, and Mr. Mathews disappeared back into his class where Zach was still writing the test I needed to pass and wasn't allowed to finish.

chapter three

I balanced my lunch tray in my hand as I slipped between the tables and chairs and bodies in the cafeteria. The table my friends and I always sat at was right in the middle. I liked being right in the middle where everything was happening, where I wouldn't miss anything.

And there was always so much going on—talking, laughing, arguments or fights, walking, moving, dancing, singing and strutting. I loved the activity in the cafeteria.

It was like I had a 3-D digital satellite TV with a thousand stations, and I just sat there clicking from station to station. I loved watching people. People were just about the most interesting thing in the world, and no two were the same. The only thing more interesting than people was lots of people.

I nodded or said hello to dozens of kids as I navigated my way through. I knew so many kids by name, or at least to nod at, that my friends always kidded me that I knew everybody at the school. That wasn't true. Nobody knew everybody, but I knew lots of people, even those in different grades.

A lot of kids in grade nine and ten are afraid of the seniors. I never was because when I was in grade nine, my big brother, James, was in grade twelve. It never hurts to have a big brother—especially one who was on the football team and school president—to keep an eye on you. I knew his friends, and sometimes they'd even let me hang with them. That was a major boost on the cool scale. It was really nice to have him around for my first year in high school.

In some ways, though, it was even nicer to not have him around this year. He was at university now—on a scholarship, of course. I hoped that teachers would stop saying things like "I taught your brother James...he was such a bright student." They never said, "And why aren't you?", but it was implied.

Cody, Devon, Ahmad, Kevin and Mohammad were already at our table, eating. I plopped down my tray. My Coke sloshed over the side of the cup and onto the table.

"This is a first," Kevin said as I sat down.

"Me spilling a Coke?"

"You late for lunch."

"I'm hoping that at least I'll be allowed to finish my lunch," I said.

"Is that why you stuck around in class? To finish your test?" Cody asked.

"I tried to finish. Mathews kicked me out. I'm ticked off."

"Since when have you ever been upset about not finishing a test?" Ahmad asked.

"Yeah, Eddie, what's the big deal?" Cody questioned.

"The big deal is that I needed to finish. Those last two or three marks might make a big difference."

"Let me get this right, you care about a couple of extra marks?" Cody said.

"Look, I'm not like you, worrying about whether you get a ninety or a ninety-two," I said. "That doesn't make any difference."

"You don't know my parents very well," he said.

"Or mine," Ahmad said. "My parents tell me that you can't become a doctor with marks in the seventies or eighties."

"Let's not even go there," I said. "The closest I'm going to get to a doctor is if I'm hit by a bus. There *is* a big difference between a forty-eight and a fifty. One is worth a credit and the other is the month of July wasted in summer school."

"Do you think you'll be that close?" Mohammed asked.

I shook my head. "Too close to call. Why does he make his tests so long that nobody can finish?"

"I finished," Cody said.

"Me too," Kevin agreed, and Mohammed nodded in agreement.

"Thanks for making me feel better."

"Why were you late anyway?" Cody asked.

"Let me guess," Kevin said. "What was her name?"

"What makes you so sure it was a girl?" I asked.

He shrugged. "Well...wasn't it?"

I smiled. "Of course, but you wouldn't know her. She's in grade twelve."

Everybody *oooed* and *awwwed*.

I knew a bunch of girls in the older grades. I figured if I was going to be rejected, I might as well be rejected by older women. If you're going to be shot down, at least aim for the stars.

"We were talking in the library. She had a spare, so when the bell went she didn't have to go," I explained.

"But you don't have a spare," Cody said.

"Thanks for pointing out the obvious. It's just that I forgot that we had a test."

"You forgot? You mean you were so distracted that it slipped your mind?" Mohammed asked.

"It sort of slipped my mind last night."

"You didn't study at all?" Mohammed sounded like he couldn't believe that was possible. "If you don't study, you'll never get a good mark."

"This is like having lunch with my mother," I joked. "Speaking of which, my parents will kill me if I flunk another test. I've got to do something."

"You could study and show up on time," Cody suggested.

"Now it's my mother *and* my father at the table. Besides, I said I had to do something, not something extreme. If I just had a little more time, I could have finished that test. Did you guys know that some people actually get more time to write tests?"

"Yeah," Cody said. "People in special-education programs."

"You knew about that?" I questioned.

He shrugged. "Don't most people know that?"

Others nodded in agreement.

"If only I was special ed, then I could still be in there and..." I stopped talking as a light went on in my head. "I think I have the solution to my problem. I have a plan."

"I can't wait to hear this," Ahmad said.

"Me neither," Kevin agreed. "Anybody want to take bets on how much trouble he's going to get in over this?"

"Hold on, you haven't even heard my plan yet."

"Don't most of your plans end with you being in trouble?" Cody asked.

"Okay, fair enough, but not this one. This one will get me out of trouble, out of tests and out of people giving me lectures."

"You're going to work harder?" Ahmad asked.

"Of course not. My solution is so much simpler. You've heard of people working smarter instead of working harder?"

Everybody nodded.

"So you're going to work smarter?"

"Actually, I'm going to work dumber."

"Haven't you been doing that already?" Kevin asked.

"That's where you're wrong. I have thus far only been, technically, a lazy underachiever. It is time for me to make a move from underachieving slacker to special education."

"What are you talking about?" Cody asked.

"I'm about to take advantage of this whole special-education scam."

"What does that mean?" Kevin questioned.

"Apparently I have to explain everything to you guys. Perhaps you are all special-education candidates...like me."

"Like you?"

"Exactly. Let me explain. I'm just sorry I can't provide you all with diagrams, maybe do a PowerPoint presentation, but I'll try to use small words and I'll talk very slowly... slowly. And for important words—or as we call them, the key words—I will raise my voice and make gestures."

"This should be good," Cody said.

"It will be very good."

"I meant that sarcastically," Cody said.

"Before, I would have understood what that word meant, but now?" I shrugged. "I have no idea what big words even mean."

"This sounds really stupid," Kevin said.

"Normally I might be offended by that— assuming I knew what *offended* meant—but not today. You see," I said and paused, "I am special."

"You're not special."

"My mother always says I'm special," I said. "Now all I have to do is convince the school that I'm special so that I can get all the extra things that the special-ed kids get."

"Like short buses and helmets?"

"I wouldn't mind a bus ride to school, but I'm talking about extra time for tests, spell-checkers, a computer and somebody to take notes for me."

"You could always take your own notes," Cody suggested, "like the rest of us do."

"I just wish I could, but I can't because of my very special needs. That's why I've never taken any notes. It's not that I don't want to...it's that I can't."

Cody laughed. "You don't take notes because you're lazy, you don't take school seriously and you don't care if you get good marks."

"Those are possible explanations, but I think I'll stick with my theory. Is there anybody here who doesn't think they could get better marks if they had all those things to help them?"

Nobody answered.

"Then you see my point."

"But you can't just decide you're special education. They have to do some testing."

"That's fine with me. I don't mind taking a test...especially one that I plan to fail. How hard is it to fail a test?"

"You've proven that it's not that hard," Cody pointed out.

"My point exactly. I've had practice at failing, so I should be able to tank any test they give me."

"But somebody has to recommend you for the testing."

"I don't think that will be much of a challenge. Like I said, I have a plan."

"Just out of curiosity, how long have you been thinking about this?" Cody asked.

I looked at my watch. "Almost two minutes."

"Don't you think a little more thought would be good?"

"I've always believed that it's best to think as little as possible."

"So, what are you going to do, just waltz into the guidance department and tell them you're special ed and need to be tested?" Cody asked.

My eyes widened and I smiled. "That's exactly what I'm going to do." I got up and grabbed my tray. "Oh, and there's one other thing. I don't want you to call me Eddy anymore."

They all looked confused.

"From now on, I'm special Ed."

chapter four

I strolled into the guidance department. The receptionist looked up from her work and gave me a big smile.

"And how are you doing today, Eddie?" she asked sweetly.

"I am so good it should be illegal."

"You always sound so positive...even when you're in trouble."

"Me, in trouble?" I asked, my eyes widening as if I was shocked. "Occasionally there are misunderstandings, but I can't honestly say I've ever been in trouble...well, not real trouble."

She slowly shook her head. It probably meant something that in a school this big the guidance department receptionist knew me by name. I'd made many trips in here for one thing or another over the past year and a half. But really, it had been more misunderstandings—me misunderstanding that they wanted me to do my work, show up on time, show respect for stupid teachers and get better marks. They were all just misunderstandings.

"So," she said, "what brings you to see us today?"

"I was hoping that Mrs. Flanagan had some time to see me."

"She's in her office. I'll see if she's free."

She picked up the phone and dialed. I could hear it ringing through the closed door of her office. Two rings and then it stopped. I could hear the muffled voices on both ends of the phone, as I was standing halfway between the receptionist and Mrs. Flanagan's office.

The door to her office opened and Mrs. Flanagan appeared. She gave me a big smile and motioned for me to come in.

As I entered, she moved a gigantic stack of papers from one chair and piled them onto a stack on the floor. Her entire office was a series of piles of paper that formed a soft sculpture. It was really a big, open filing cabinet where she kept everything she needed.

"So, what happened?" she asked as I sat down.

"Why does everybody think that something bad has happened?"

"The best indicator of what is going to happen in the future is to look at what has happened in the past."

"What?" I questioned.

"Usually you're here because you've gotten yourself in trouble with one of the teachers."

"Couldn't I just be here to say hello to my favorite guidance counselor?" I asked. "Couldn't I just be here to see how you're doing because I care?"

"I'm touched that you care, and it's so nice to say hello. So, what happened?"

"Nothing...well, nothing much. I was late for math class today."

"Kids don't generally see me because they were late for class, or I'd have a lineup right out the door and down the hall."

"It wasn't that. It was the test."

"You had a test today?" she asked, sounding a little more concerned.

"I had most of a test today. I couldn't finish it."

"Coming in late when you have a test isn't wise."

"I know that," I agreed. "It's like I know I have to go through that door and sit down and write it, and I just can't do it...it's like... no, this is stupid...I shouldn't be wasting your time."

I went to get up, and she reached over and placed a hand on my arm. "This is not stupid, and you're not wasting my time. Please go on."

I settled back into my seat and took a deep breath for dramatic effect.

"It's just that when I know I have to take a test, I get all uneasy...I have to fight the urge to run away." I paused. "Isn't that stupid?"

"It's not stupid. It sounds like you really have a phobia around taking tests."

"A what?"

"A phobia. Nobody likes taking tests, but some people are physically upset by them. I know some people who actually throw up before they take a test."

"I do feel sick to my stomach sometimes," I said. I wasn't even lying—but didn't tests make everybody feel that way?

"And I know I need to get there on time to have any hope of finishing the test," I said.

She gave me a questioning look.

"I don't finish a lot of tests," I said.

"I didn't know that."

"Yeah. I figure my marks would be higher if I had time to do all the questions. But, what can you do? I guess I'll just have to stop being upset about taking tests, because when I screw up it makes me look stupid."

"You're not stupid!" she protested.

"You couldn't tell that by looking at my report cards."

"Report cards aren't a complete indication of intelligence."

"You want to tell that to my teachers and parents?" I suggested.

"I think they know that."

"I'm pretty sure they think I'm stupid."

"Please, let's not use that word anymore," she suggested.

"Not using it is easy. Not believing it is harder. I better get going or I'll be late for English."

"I'd like you to come and see me again after school," Mrs. Flanagan suggested.

"Why?"

"I want to talk to you more about your test phobia. Perhaps we could do something about it."

"What sort of something?"

"Perhaps if we did some testing—"

"Testing? Weren't you listening?" I asked. "I don't like tests!"

"But it's to see if perhaps you need additional—"

"I gotta go!"

I rushed out of her office, through the guidance department and out into the hall before she could say anything else.

Safely away, I let a little smile creep onto my face. She wanted me tested, and I'd played hard to get. I was sure that she wouldn't just let me walk away. She would track me down or maybe even contact my parents. Step one was complete.

chapter five

I threw my books into my locker, grabbed my jacket and slammed the locker closed.

"You ready?" I asked Cody.

"Almost. I've just got to grab my history book."

"History? We don't have a test, do we?" I questioned.

"No, but we do have pages to read. Chapter three, remember?"

"Yeah, sure," I said. Actually I didn't remember. "I'll do it tomorrow at lunch."

"But tomorrow is day one of a new cycle—we have history before lunch tomorrow."

"Oh yeah, that's right. The way our schedule rotates never makes sense to me."

"It's not that hard. You just have to remember that we're on a six-day cycle and—"

"Yeah, yeah, I know." I opened up my locker and dug around until I found the history textbook.

"There is a test on Friday," Cody said. "You could start studying tonight."

I shook my head. "That wouldn't work. Anything I crammed into my head tonight would be gone by Friday. I'll do my studying Thursday night."

"Really?"

"There's always a chance."

"Coming down the hall to your left," Cody whispered.

I started to turn my head to look, and he poked me in the shoulder. I shot him a dirty look—what was he doing?

"Don't be so obvious," he hissed.

Slowly, casually, I looked down the hall. Of course, I could immediately see what he was referring to. Elizabeth and a couple of her friends were walking toward us...well, not really toward us, just in our direction.

Her two friends, Jen and Sarah, were cute enough, but they were, at least to me, almost lost in her glow.

"Don't stare, and close your mouth," Cody whispered.

I was going to argue, but instead I closed my mouth and tried not to stare. That wasn't easy. Elizabeth was nothing short of perfect. She had long flowing blond hair, curves in just the right places, beautiful blue eyes and perfect skin. The way she moved was...well...breathtaking. Watching her walk was like seeing a shampoo commercial. Actually she had been in a shampoo commercial. She did some modeling. I heard it was mainly for catalogs and some stuff in TV commercials as well.

They passed by. I tried to give her a nod and a smile, but none of them even saw us. Apparently I'd mastered the superhero ability to become invisible. X-ray vision would have worked much better...what was she wearing underneath that sweater?

I continued to watch as she walked away. She was almost as good moving away as she'd been walking toward us—and I didn't have to worry about her seeing me staring.

"I thought she was away today," Cody said.

I gave him a questioning look.

"You're not the only one who notices her," he explained. "She wasn't in class today for the math test."

"Yeah, that's right," I said. I was so occupied with the test that I hadn't even noticed. Now that was just plain sad.

"I wonder why she wasn't there," he said.

"I figure if you're that beautiful, you don't have to take tests," I sighed.

"Could be," he agreed.

The girls made the turn at the end of the hall and disappeared.

"So, what's happening with your latest plan?" Cody asked.

"Working it through. Tell me, what do you know about special education?"

"Enough to know that you should want to avoid it."

"What's wrong with being special ed?"

"You don't really want to be one of those kids, do you?"

"If you mean one of those kids who get extra time for tests, then the answer is yes."

"But what will people think about you?" Cody asked.

"Since when have I ever cared what people think?"

"How about people like Elizabeth?" he asked.

"She won't care if I'm in special ed," I said.

"Actually, you're right."

I gave him a questioning look. "Why the sudden turn around?"

"She'd have to know who you are to care," Cody said.

"She knows who I am."

"Yeah, right."

"We are in the same math class, remember?" I asked.

"Yeah, and that's all you two will ever share."

"A guy has to dream. Besides, she wouldn't know. I didn't know anything about Zach."

"That's only because you don't pay attention."

We walked out the front door. Lots of kids streamed out of the school with us, heading for the parking lot or the bus stop.

"There's my mother," I said. "I'll see you later."

"Wait!" Cody said, as he grabbed my arm.

"What? Do you need a ride home?"

"No, I just want you to be careful."

"Come on, my mom's not that bad a driver."

"I mean, your idea about becoming special ed...don't do anything stupid."

"You obviously have to get with the plan. My idea *is* to do something stupid...well, exceptional, I guess, really. Later."

My mother was in our SUV, circling the parking lot. I ran along, waving my arms, and she saw me and pulled over.

"How was your day?" she asked as soon as I settled in.

"Not bad. How about yours?"

"Busy, but good. Thanks for asking."

We pulled away and she wove through the waiting cars and joined the line to exit the parking lot. It was always busy, our own little rush hour. I couldn't wait to join it as a driver instead of a passenger. Getting a ride home was certainly better than walking or taking a bus, but it was seriously uncool to be picked up by your mommy.

In three more months, I'd be sixteen and could drive myself. That is, if I could bring my marks up. My parents had made it clear that I had to get better grades if I wanted use of the car.

They probably should have been more specific about what they meant by better. Sixty was better than fifty-five so technically that would be better. But maybe I could get out of even doing that—time to continue the plan.

"Can we eat early tonight?" I asked.

"I imagine we can."

"Good. I have a lot of studying to do." I held up my history book to show Exhibit A.

"Do you have a test tomorrow?" She sounded concerned. She was always much more worried about my tests than I was.

"No, the test is on Thursday."

"And you're going to start studying tonight?" Instead of worried, she sounded confused...maybe a little bit shocked.

"Don't sound so surprised. I do study, you know."

"Sorry, I didn't mean it that way."

"What do you think I do when I'm in my room?" I asked.

"Well, I see you watching TV and playing video games, and I hear you talking on the phone and listening to music."

"That's how I study. It's called multitasking."

"I could never study like that," my mother said.

"That's because you're old...I mean older."

She'd started to give me a dirty look, but those extra two letters took care of that—nice save.

It was funny, but I was often happiest when I was doing two or three things at once. I guess I could study in silence...no, that sounded boring.

"Most successful people know how to multitask. Isn't your office busy and noisy?"

"My office is always buzzing. People talking, yelling, laughing, and phones ringing."

"Then it sounds like you do work like that. Not only can you work like a teenager, but you still look like a teenager."

She shook her head slowly. My mother knew when I was conning her, but still a little smile came to her face.

"Three nights of studying should help you get a good mark on that test."

"You'd think," I said. "I just hope that's the way it was with my math test today."

"You had a math test today?" she asked—there was that concern again. She sounded super-serious.

"Yeah. A hard one. A long one."

"And how do you think you did?" she asked.

"I think I passed. Barely. Maybe. I would have done better if I could have finished."

"You didn't finish?"

"I ran out of time, and my teacher told me I had to hand it in."

"Your teacher wouldn't let you finish your test?" She spun around in her seat to face me with such force that the car swerved into the next lane. The car that she'd cut off honked its horn.

"Eyes front!" I yelled. "Let's just start off by getting home in one piece."

"Why wouldn't he let you finish your test?"

"The period was over, and I couldn't get it all done. I asked for more time, but he said no."

"As soon as I get home, I'm going to call the school and give him a piece of my—"

"No!" I exclaimed, cutting her off—hopefully in word and action. It was always best to keep parents and teachers from talking. Especially when the teacher could tell the parent that I showed up nearly twenty minutes late for this particular test.

"I wasn't going to tell him off. I just wanted to talk to him about giving you more time."

"It wouldn't do any good."

"But if a parent asked him, he'd surely let you have longer."

"No, he wouldn't."

"Then he isn't a very good teacher."

"He's actually a great teacher."

"Well, then he doesn't sound very fair."

"It is fair and it's not his fault. He's just following the rules. Everybody gets the same time to complete tests." I paused. "Well, everybody but the special-education kids. They get as much time as they need."

"They do?"

"They do," I said. "But that's only fair too. If they need more time then they should get it."

I looked at the back of the car in front of us—there was a bumper sticker. Oh perfect. I didn't know much about learning problems, but I knew that some people read words backward.

"That is so funny!" I said.

"What's so funny?"

"Look at the bumper sticker on that car ahead of us!"

"I see it...but what's so funny?" she asked.

"They must be real animal people."

"What do you mean?" she questioned.

"Well, really, *Dog is Great* is a strange thing to put on your bumper."

"*Dog is Great*? No," my mother said, "it says *God is Great*."

"No, it says *dog*...wait...I guess it does say *God*. I guess I just wasn't reading it right."

"You read the letters backward."

"Not all of them!" I protested. "Just the one word, and it was just for a second."

"I see," she said. "You know you used to do that all the time."

"Did what all the time?"

"Reverse letters. You did that a lot when you were learning to read."

"Doesn't everybody?"

"Yes, I suppose."

We drove in silence for a while, but I knew that silence wasn't going to last long.

"Does that happen much?" she asked.

"Does what happen much?" I asked.

"The bumper sticker."

"I don't know...I guess lots of people think God is great. It certainly makes more sense than thinking that dog is—"

"I meant, reversing the letters."

"Not really...hardly ever."

"But it does happen?" she pressed.

"Occasionally. You know, if I'm rushed or things are too hectic. Sometimes I still write the number three backward."

"Really?"

"Occasionally. It's no big deal."

We pulled into our driveway, and I took off my seatbelt and quickly climbed out before my mother could ask me any more questions. I'd already given her the answers I wanted her to hear.

chapter six

The door was opened by a middle-aged woman. She was well-dressed and attractive—for a woman that age.

"Hello, I'm Dr. McClintock," she said as she extended her hand to shake.

"I'm Edward," I said. "I wasn't expecting a doctor. Should I call you Doctor or what?"

"You can if you want. Many people just call me Ellen. How about if you call me Ellen and I'll call you Edward...or do your friends call you Ed?"

"Sometimes Ed, sometimes Eddy." I left out Fast Eddy.

"Which do you prefer?"

"Either is good."

"Well then, hello, Ed. Please come into my office."

"Thanks, Ellen."

I walked in. The room was cozy.

"Have a seat," she said.

I headed toward a chair in front of the big desk.

"No, please, let's sit here." She gestured to three large leather chairs around a little coffee table. I sank into one of the seats. It was big and soft and very comfortable. She sat on the chair right beside me.

The walls of the office were lined with shelves of books. There were pictures on the walls along with a number of diplomas— just to prove she was a doctor and not a plumber. Maybe plumbers had certificates as well, although I imagine that they'd be different than those that a—

"This is very unusual that I see somebody so quickly after a referral is made," she said.

"Quickly? It's been almost three weeks."

She laughed. "Often it's three or four months. There was a cancellation—the student I was supposed to see moved—and your guidance counselor was most insistent that I see you."

"Mrs. Flanagan can be pretty insistent."

"As can your parents." She paused. "You know, of course, that I've met with your parents."

"They told me."

"And that's okay with you?" she asked.

I shrugged. "Why wouldn't it be all right with me? I've got nothing to hide."

"That's a good attitude," she said.

"What other attitude could I have?"

"Some students are resistant, even upset and angry. Some refuse to talk to me."

"Why wouldn't they want to talk to you?"

"Some kids don't want to be thought of as having difficulties."

"Not me. I figure you're only here to help me."

She smiled. "I'm glad you feel that way. You don't have anything to be nervous about."

"I'm not nervous." Actually I was a little nervous. Maybe I couldn't pull this off.

"Not even a little nervous?"

I shook my head.

"It's just that you're leg is twitching. That's often a sign of nervousness."

I looked down at my leg like it was a stranger to me. I hadn't noticed, but if twitching showed I was nervous, I'd put on a personal earthquake of movement.

I'd been doing a lot of reading, trying to decide what special-education thing I was going to become. I'd read about hyperactivity. This was something I could easily do—at least to start.

There were, in fact, thousands of exceptionalities. I figured the safest thing to do was have a whole bunch of them. It was the shotgun approach to special education.

"I'll try not to be nervous. I just have trouble sitting still," I said.

"That's pretty common," she said.

Common? I didn't want common, I wanted exceptional. "I had a kindergarten teacher who said I had ants in my pants. At the time I found that very confusing and a little bit scary." I started to tap my fingers against the side of the chair, doing my own little drum solo.

"Do you ever have trouble concentrating?" she asked.

"What?" I asked, pretending I didn't hear the question.

"Concentrating...do you have trouble concentrating?" she repeated.

"Not really, I guess. That's a nice picture," I said, pointing to one of the paintings.

"Yes, it's one of my favorites as well. Sometimes I just sit here and—"

"How long have you been doing this?"

"I've been a psychologist for almost twenty years."

"So you must be pretty good at it."

"I certainly try. Again, are you feeling nervous about this assess—"

"Do you want some gum?" I asked, cutting her off again. I whipped a package out of my pocket and offered it to her.

"I'm fine, but thank you for offering."

"No problem. Did you always want to be a psychologist when you were growing up?"

"Not always. Do you ever think about what you want to be?"

"I think about it, but really, unless I can get my marks up, it doesn't matter what I want to be, because I won't be able to become anything."

"That must be troubling."

"Sometimes. You sure you don't want any gum?"

"Positive."

She picked up a file folder from the little table and opened it.

"This is the test you completed."

"I hope I did okay. I hope I passed."

"There's no passing or failing in a questionnaire."

"That's good to know. Tests make me nervous." Test anxiety was one of the things

I was hoping to fake—actually I wasn't faking that much.

"I noticed a number of letter reversals on your questionnaire."

"Really?" I asked innocently. There were actually thirty-two—I'd counted them as I deliberately made them. Dyslexia seemed pretty easy to fake.

"Yes, there are many reversals, including something I don't think I've ever seen before."

"What's that?" I asked.

She turned the sheet so I could see it. "I don't think I've ever seen a reversal in somebody's name."

I faked a look of shock. Edward was written with the first *d* reversed.

"I guess I was a little more nervous than I thought. Do you want me to fix it?"

"Is this a common problem for you?" she asked.

I leaned in closer. "If I don't concentrate really, really hard," I said, my voice just above a whisper, "then it can happen a lot. Sometimes I'm so busy making sure the letters or numbers are the right way that I can't even figure out if it's the right answer."

"That must make taking tests very hard."

"Very." I paused. "You know..." I paused again. "I really do like that picture." I pointed to the painting above her head.

"I'm glad you like it. Is there anything else you'd like to share?"

I shook my head. "Not that I can think of...or remember. You know, sometimes my memory isn't the best." I'd read that there were three types of memory—long-term, mid-term, and I couldn't remember the third...no wait, it was short-term memory.

"Then we'll just get on with the testing," she said.

"That's good. The sooner we start, the sooner we end. How long is this going to take?"

"We're going to have three sessions, each about three hours long."

"Wow," I said—thinking both that it was long, and that if I spelled the word *wow* backward it would still be *wow*, and *mom* would still be *mom*. Unless I spun them upside down, and then *wow* would be *mom* and *mom* would be *wow* and—

"Of course, we're not going to do all of your testing this week."

"Oh yeah, that's right. I was told, but I guess it slipped my mind." I tried not to smile—a few more seeds planted in the poor memory category.

"Because of that cancellation, we'll be able to do the first three-hour session today, and then we'll have to wait until there's another opening. It could be two or three more weeks. I hope that isn't a problem?"

"Not for me. Do you want some...wait, I already offered you gum, didn't I?"

She nodded.

"I guess we should just get on with the testing," I said.

"Yes, let's get started," Ellen said.

chapter seven

"You're very quiet," my mother said as we drove home.

"I'm just a little tired. That was incredibly long."

"You were in there for close to four hours. What exactly did they have you do?"

"Some of it was just talking," I said.

"I like that Dr. McClintock."

"Yeah, Ellen's nice."

"Ellen?"

"That's what she told me to call her. She asked lots of questions. Sometimes it was things like her saying a series of words and having me repeat them back."

"Interesting."

"Sort of boring, but it was easy enough."

"And what wasn't so easy?"

"The written part. It was really, really long. Some of the questions were like little essays, and some of the multiple-choice questions were just plain strange."

"What sort of questions?"

"Like if I was a bed wetter, if I was cruel to animals or if I heard voices."

"I thought those were a bit strange myself," my mother agreed.

"You saw the test?"

"Not the one you took, but your father and I had to fill out a long questionnaire as well. There were over two hundred questions."

"And what did you tell them?" I asked.

"Well, of course we told them that you don't wet the bed and you're very good to our pets and—"

"And I don't hear voices. I know all that. But what did you tell them about me?"

"We said you were a very nice young man, who had lots of friends—sometimes too many friends—who liked sports, had lots of activities, had a great sense of humor and was smart."

I liked all of those answers except for the smart part. I was working hard to prove to them that I was exceptional, not smart.

"If I'm so smart, how come my reports are always so bad?" I asked.

"I don't think that has to do with your intelligence."

"It doesn't have anything to do with my shoe size," I said.

"The purpose of this testing is to find out why our smart son doesn't get the marks that he should."

The normal assumption was that I was slacking off, lazy, not trying, not studying, not taking school seriously and underachieving. This was definitely showing signs of progress.

"We did write that you've always been a very active child," my mother said.

"Almost *hyper*active."

She turned slightly in her seat and gave me a questioning look.

"Hyperactive...isn't that what they call kids who can't sit still?" I said.

"Your father always says that he could never sit still as a child either," my mother said. "And we did mention the letter reversals."

"Yeah, I told her about that too."

"Good for you for being honest," she said. "That's one of the other things we mentioned, that you are a very trustworthy and honest young man."

"Thanks." I suddenly felt very guilty. Here I was, trying to fool my parents, the school and the psychologist. That didn't sound so honest.

For a microsecond, I wondered if I should just confess. I tried to imagine just how much trouble that would get me in. I couldn't do that. And really, who was this going to hurt? If I got extra time and extra help, my marks would improve. That would make my parents happy. That would make the school happy. So really, if you thought about it, I was doing this for them.

Wow...it was truly amazing how I could convince myself of almost anything if I needed to.

chapter eight

I nibbled on my sandwich, trying to act like I wasn't listening as Ahmad and Kevin threw questions back and forth at each other. They knew their stuff. It was evident that they'd both studied for the history test. What was becoming more obvious—but only to me—was that I knew my stuff too. Maybe I didn't know it the way they did. Ahmad was like a walking, talking textbook, but I knew as much as Kevin did.

I'd done something unusual. I'd studied for the test. I'd left the TV off, shut down my computer, turned off my cell phone and studied. I had only a little music in the background, and when that got too distracting, I'd turned it down.

Cody walked up and joined us. He threw out an answer to one of their questions, and the two of them gave him a little high five. Cody turned to me.

"You know there's a history test next period, right?"

"Well, I know now," I said. "I didn't think that these two just like quizzing each other on American history."

"I tried to call you last night to remind you," he said.

"I looked for you on MSN, but you weren't there," Kevin added.

"I had better things to do." The better thing was studying. I needed to pass this test to pass the term.

"What was her name?" Cody asked.

"A gentleman never tells."

"That's why I'm asking you."

"You are hilarious."

"Thank you," Cody said.

"And it's not just my opinion," I added. "I was listening to a bunch of the girls talking about you."

"About me?" he questioned. "Who was it?"

"Elizabeth and her friends."

"Elizabeth?" he gasped. "What did she say?"

"I'll see if I can remember the exact words..."

"What? What did she say?"

"She said, 'That Cody is such a funny guy.'"

"Really?"

"Yeah, funny...funny *looking*...she said she laughed whenever she saw you...she thought you were a joke."

He looked crushed, and I instantly felt bad.

"Cody, I'm joking."

"I knew that," he said.

"Elizabeth wouldn't say any of those things about you," I said, and he looked reassured. "I doubt she even knows who you are." That was the truth.

"Like she knows you either," Cody said.

"She knows me."

"Don't flatter yourself," Ahmad said.

"She does. I've actually had conversations with her...unlike anybody else at this table."

"Asking her if you can borrow a pencil isn't exactly a conversation," Cody said.

"It's a conversation starter," I said. "I'm working my way into a conversation, taking my time. You know, playing hard to get."

"Yeah, I'm sure that's working," Kevin said. "She's probably lying awake at night dreaming about you."

"Of course not," I said. "You can't be awake and dreaming."

I had to admit that she was a little bit intimidating. Besides being spectacularly beautiful and a part-time model, she was a serious student, and her boyfriends were usually in grade twelve—and big.

"I'd ask her out, but I'm not sure she's my type," I said.

"Yeah, right!" Kevin scoffed, and the others hooted in agreement. "So, what exactly is your type?"

"Yeah, I want to hear this," Ahmad agreed.

"Well...first off...I really like them to be desperate."

"Desperate?"

"Yeah, and have low standards. The lower, the better," I added, and everybody laughed. "And if they're blind, that's good too, and—"

The bell rang, cutting me off. We gathered up our stuff as everybody else in the cafeteria did the same. The sound of hundreds of chairs simultaneously scraping against the floor sent a chill up my spine. We had five minutes to get to class.

We shuffled our way through the maze of tables, chairs and kids. Ahmad and Kevin kept throwing questions at each other, yelling out the answers over the roar of the crowd. There was a question that I didn't know the answer to, and I turned around—Kevin didn't know it either.

"Well?" I asked Ahmad.

"Seventeen ninety-two in Philadephia."

"Are you sure?" Kevin asked.

"Look who you're talking to," he said.

I had to agree. If he'd said 1792 on Mars, I would have believed him.

"Thanks. I'll see you guys later," I said.

As I started to walk away Cody grabbed me by the arm and spun me around.

"Where do you think you're going?" he asked. "History is this way."

"I know where the class is. I'm going this way," I said, pointing in the opposite direction.

"Come on, Eddy, just come to class. You have to take the test," he said.

Ahmad and Kevin both looked worried.

"It's okay," I reassured them. "I am going to take the test."

"We want you to start it on time so you'll pass," Ahmad said.

"I'll pass and I will start on time. I'm just not starting in the same place as the rest of you."

They all gave me a questioning look.

"I'm taking the test in the special-education room."

"You've been designated special ed?" Kevin gasped.

"Not yet. They still have some testing to do, but they're letting me work there on a trial basis."

"Wow," Kevin said. "I can't believe that you did it...you fooled them."

"It wasn't hard."

"You're, like, a genius," Ahmad said. He sounded impressed.

"An evil genius," Cody said.

"There's nothing evil about this. Nobody gets hurt. Besides, I don't want any more talk about me being a genius. I'm just Ed...special Ed." I paused. "By the way, I probably won't see you guys in fifth period. I get twice as long for this test, so I'm probably not going to get around to math." I looked at my watch. "You better get going. Only one of us can afford to be late for this test."

I turned and walked away.

chapter nine

I hesitated at the door of the support room. This was the first time I'd been down here. The door was slightly ajar. I pushed it open a little more and looked inside. The room was ringed with computers. In the middle were tables and chairs—some of them were leathery-looking lounge chairs. There were a couple of overstuffed sofas. The room had fluorescent overhead lights like every class in the school, but they were turned off. Instead the room was lit with small table lights. It was softer and easier on the eyes. There was music quietly coming from a CD player sitting on the counter. It was the wordless elevator music that my parents liked. No words, no beat, no nothing.

If it wasn't for the computers, this room would have seemed more like a living room than a classroom. It looked very inviting, like the room was welcoming me, wanting me to come in...but should I really go in? Should I really be here?

"Excuse me."

I startled as a guy—a big guy, maybe in grade twelve—pushed by me into the room. He was quickly followed by another guy and a couple of girls.

"Hello, Edward."

I turned around. It was Miss Manning, one of the special-ed teachers.

"It's so good to see you!" she exclaimed.

She was one of the happiest people I'd ever met. She was always cheerful. You'd think that all those special-ed kids might have worn that out of her, but that wasn't the case.

"Are you going in?"

"Yes, right, of course," I stammered. We both walked into the room.

"Where should I sit?"

"You can sit anywhere you want, but since you're here to take a test it might be better for you to sit at a table."

"Yeah, right."

"And I have your test right here."

She opened a large brown envelope and pulled out my test, putting it down on the table in front of me.

"Now remember that you have lots of time," she said.

"Twice as long as normal—right?"

"If you have any questions, you just have to ask."

"Right...thanks."

"I'll be working with other students, but tests always have priority. Just call and I'll come and help."

"Great, thanks."

I took a deep breath and then picked up the test. It was three sheets, stapled together. The first page was multiple-choice questions. I liked multiple-choice. Even a monkey making random choices was guaranteed to get about one out of four of them right.

I flipped to the next page. True-and-false questions! I loved true-or-false. That same monkey could get half of them right. I could be that monkey.

I turned to the last page. It was essay questions. They weren't my favorite, but I could usually bluff my way enough to get at least part marks.

This wasn't looking so bad at all. In fact it was a very, very short test. I wasn't going to need extra time. In fact, if every test was this long, I'd never need extra time.

I planned to work fast, finish up and then leave and go to the cafeteria—my math teacher would assume that I was still in the support room. That was a plan... no wait...bad plan. The first time in the support room, I needed to take all the time I could—at least the same time as everybody else and then at least half as much and—

"Ed, are you having difficulties?" Miss Manning asked.

I startled. "No, I'm okay."

"I noticed you hadn't started."

"I just wanted to look it over first before I started to write," I explained.

"That is so smart!" she exclaimed. "Any questions so far?"

"I haven't put down my name, so I think up to this point I'm okay."

"I'll let you get back to work."

I looked at the first question and the potential answers. I had a little rush of anxiety as I realized that the answer wasn't coming. I'd actually studied for this test and I still didn't know the answer. Maybe I really was special education!

Okay, slow down, don't be stupid— I wasn't stupid. I could do this. All I had to do was think, and I had all the time I wanted to think. And if I still didn't know, I could ask Miss Manning for help. She wouldn't give me the answers, but she could help me figure them out—that was why she was here. That was why I was here.

I took a deep breath and looked at the answers again. I was able to eliminate three answers quickly. Two could be the right one, but there was definitely one that was more right. I circled that answer. That felt good. I could do this.

I'd finished up pretty quickly. It was early enough that I could have gone straight to math. But that wasn't the plan. Not only because I really didn't want to go to math, but because I had to make sure I looked special ed.

That was part of the reason I'd studied so hard. I wanted them to see the improvement in my marks. They'd think it was because I was getting this support—that I was special education.

Not that I was going to keep studying. That would defeat the purpose of making my life easier. Right now it was short-term pain for long-term gain. Once everybody knew I belonged here, then I'd go back to my normal study habits.

I'd finished the test and even checked the answers, but I still had time to kill. I looked around. There were ten other kids in the room. I didn't know any of them, but I recognized a couple of them from around the school. Some of them looked pretty normal. A few really looked special education—the sort of kid who might as well have been wearing a helmet.

I didn't need the helmet, but I did want the benefits. Before, if I got a sixty, everybody thought I was a lazy underachiever. Now they'd think I was a plucky fighter, battling my learning problems. There was no downside to this.

The door opened and Elizabeth walked in! I almost dropped my pencil. What was she doing in here? The last thing I wanted was for her to think that I was special education. There'd be absolutely no chance of her ever wanting to have anything to do with me!

"Hello, Elizabeth!" Miss Manning called out.

"Hi, Miss Manning. Sorry I'm late, but I had to pick up the assignment from my science teacher. I'm hoping you can help me understand the section on genetics."

"That's why we're here, to help."

I practically gasped. That was why Elizabeth was here—she was special education! I didn't know anybody who would have argued about the special part, but I'd just thought she was special as in perfect.

She looked over in my direction, and I quickly looked down at my paper so she wouldn't know that I'd been staring at her. I didn't want to embarrass either of us.

This was unbelievable. As soon as she started to work, I'd just slip out of the room. In the meantime, I'd check my test—again.

Question by question I worked my way through the test, making sure I hadn't missed a question or answered wrong. This was really a pain, but there was no choice. It looked good. I wasn't going to just squeak by, but pass with flying colors. This was going to remove any doubt that with support I could do a lot better. I'd been in here long enough. I could now leave.

I looked over at Elizabeth. She had her back to me, still working on her test. Quietly I got up. So quiet and careful not to disturb anybody—as in Elizabeth—I padded over and handed the test to Miss Manning.

"You're all finished?" she asked.

"Yeah, all done," I whispered.

"Good."

I took another glance at Elizabeth. She was working away, oblivious to me. I started for the door. Leaving here didn't mean I had to go to math right away. I'd take a detour through the cafeteria and—

"Ed!" Miss Manning yelled.

I skidded to a stop and shuddered. So much for the silent exit. I turned around. Everybody in the room was looking at me, including Elizabeth. Miss Manning motioned for me to come over.

"Your test," she said, holding it up. "You have to finish it."

"I did finish it. I checked three times. Every question completed."

"Every question on the front of each page."

"The front?"

She held up the test. Slowly she turned over the completed first page. On the back was a fresh set of questions that I hadn't seen! My mouth dropped open in shock. I'd somehow missed a page! She flipped to the second page and there was a back to that page that I hadn't seen, and the third page was the same. I'd written only half of the test!

I felt like somebody had kicked me in the stomach.

"I...I...I can't believe it," I stammered.

"It happens. Don't worry."

"Don't worry...but I can't pass if I only wrote half the test."

"You still have time to write the rest of the test. It'll be okay."

I took the test from her and numbly walked back to the desk. So much for passing with flying colors. I guess all I could hope for was going back to barely passing.

chapter ten

"Ed...it's time."

"What?" I asked as I looked up from my test.

"The bell rang."

I was so absorbed in my test I hadn't even heard it.

"Your time is up," Miss Manning said.

"I'm almost finished."

"Almost will have to be good enough."

I looked down at the test. I was two questions away from being done. I would have been done if I hadn't wasted so much time. I wanted to blame somebody—who did two-sided tests anyway?—but I knew only one person was responsible. Yelling at myself would make me a little more special education than I wanted.

I handed her the test.

"What class did you miss to write this test?" she asked.

"Math."

"You need to go to math and find out what work you missed."

"I can tell him."

My head swiveled around. It was Elizabeth.

"We're in the same class, and I spoke to our teacher earlier today to ask him about our work for the day," she said.

"And you wouldn't mind sharing that with Ed?"

"No, I can help."

"Do either of you have any place you need to go right after school?" Miss Manning asked.

"I have time," Elizabeth said.

"Me too."

"Excellent."

"Why don't you come over here," Miss Manning said, patting the seat beside Elizabeth.

I walked slowly, feeling self-conscious. I took a seat beside her at the little study table, accidentally bumping into her leg as I settled in. Smooth move. At least I hadn't tripped on the walk over.

"I'm Ed."

"I know."

"You do?"

"You are in my math class. It's not like your name hasn't come up, and we have talked before," she said.

If "talked" involved me mumbling hello and borrowing pencils, then we'd had repeated conversations.

"I didn't know you came here," I said.

"You didn't notice that I'm not in class a lot of the time?"

"I just thought you were someplace else...I heard you did modeling, and I figured that was where you were."

She laughed. "I did a few little things over the last year or so. If I was modeling all the time I've been here, I'd be rich."

"I just didn't know you came here."

"It's not like I announce it," she said. "I didn't know you came here either."

"I don't...I mean I never have before...this was my first time."

"So you were just designated special education?"

"Actually I'm not special ed."

She gave me a confused look.

"I mean I'm not yet. I'm here on a trial basis until they get back the test results."

"What do you think your disability is?" she asked.

"I'm not sure. I guess I'll know when they tell me. How about you?"

"I have a short-term-memory processing issue."

"Oh," I said, nodding.

"Do you know what that means?"

"No idea whatsoever."

"With most people, if you tell them something, they remember most of what you said right away and then less and less as time goes on."

"That makes sense."

"But with me it's the opposite. I remember more thirty minutes later than I do right away. It takes a long time for things to sink in."

"Now that sounds like me."

She laughed. Good sign.

"I was a little surprised to see you in here," I said.

"You were?"

I nodded. "You just seem so...so smart."

"Just because you're here doesn't mean you're not smart," she said. She sounded offended.

"I didn't mean anything bad," I apologized.

"You ever heard of a guy named Albert Einstein?"

"Of course."

"Would you say he was smart?" Elizabeth asked.

"He was a genius," I said.

"If he was in this school today, he'd be in special ed."

I gave her a look of disbelief.

"Do you know that Einstein dropped

out of high school and failed his university entrance exam?"

"I didn't know that."

"What about Leonardo da Vinci, Edison, Winston Churchill and John F. Kennedy?"

"What about them?"

"They were all learning disabled."

"Wow, I didn't know."

"It's not unusual," she said. "Lots of people who are really amazing in one area are learning disabled in another."

"And then there's those of us who aren't amazing in any area but are learning disabled as well," I said.

"Don't sell yourself short. I'm sure you're good at lots of things."

I was just about to suggest that it might be dancing, dating or making-out when Miss Manning reappeared with the photocopied work.

"So, let me show you what you're missing," Elizabeth said.

Looking at her I knew exactly what I was missing, but I guess we'd have to do the math instead.

chapter eleven

I took a seat at the end of the long table. My mother sat on one side of me and my father on the other. Stretched out along both sides of the table were my teachers, the principal and the vice-principal, and Mrs. Flanagan, my guidance counselor. At the far end sat Miss Manning and Ellen, the psychologist.

I'd been receiving unofficial support for the past three weeks. Last week I had completed the final part of the testing.

Today we'd hear the results. Either I was going to stay in the support program and continue to spend quality time with Elizabeth—a major bonus—or I was going to be tossed back into the regular class. I hoped that wasn't the case. I would miss the special support room, and extra time, and Miss Manning and all the other little perks of being special.

But that wasn't going to happen. I'd blown that psychological assessment so badly there was no way they could consider me anything else except special education. They might have to invent a whole new category of special education to explain how badly I had done.

"Good morning," Mr. MacDonald, the principal, said. "Thank you all for taking time to attend this meeting."

People mumbled out greetings.

"The purpose of this meeting, as we all know, is to discuss a possible designation of special education for Ed. Perhaps we should begin with his teachers."

"How about if I start," Mr. Hendricks, my history teacher, said.

Nobody objected. I knew Hendricks didn't like me much, but there was no point in me objecting.

"As you are all aware, Ed has not been doing very well in my class," he began.

I wondered if was too late to object.

"He rarely completes his homework. He comes to class unprepared, fails to do the assigned readings and, I feel, has always blown off my tests by doing absolutely no studying. We are all aware that he is in danger of failing my course."

"I wasn't aware of that," my father chimed in.

"This was on the midterm report," Mr. Hendricks said.

"A report that I haven't seen," my father said. He turned to me. "Edward, did you bring that report home or—?"

"I've seen it," my mother said sheepishly. "You were on a business trip when Ed brought it home."

"Well, I've been home for two weeks and I still haven't seen it."

Great, just what I wanted—a battle between the two of them in the middle of this meeting. "She probably just forgot," I said. "You get busy and she gets busy."

"Is there anything else on that midterm that I should know about?" my father questioned.

"I'm passing everything," I said to my father.

"Passing or barely passing?" he asked.

"A pass is a pass," I said.

"Which is better than last term," my mother offered.

"Certainly during the second term there has been some improvement," the principal said diplomatically.

"I'm afraid I'd have to disagree with that," Mr. Hendricks said, and everybody turned to him.

"I have Ed's most recent test," he said, holding it up. "The first test he has taken while receiving support. Calling the results of this test some improvement would be completely wrong."

My heart sank. I'd really tried to do well

on that test. I'd studied, and I'd been in the support room and had even gone over the whole thing twice. I could understand doing badly if Miss Manning hadn't caught the fact that I'd missed writing half the test, but I did write it—all except for two questions.

"What was the mark?" my father asked.

"Forty-five...out of fifty," Mr. Hendricks said. "This is not *some* improvement. This is a ninety percent, which is almost forty percent higher than his last test!"

He stood up, reached out his hand and we shook hands as there was a round of applause in the room.

"It looks like the extra support really paid off!" Miss Manning said. She came around the table and gave me a little hug, and my father gave me a pat on the back.

"And I think I owe Ed an apology," Mr. Hendricks said.

"An apology?" I gasped. "For what?"

"For thinking that you were just slacking off when you were doing the best that you could."

"Maybe I wasn't doing exactly the best I could do," I stammered.

"Obviously you needed some support. Now that support is in place, I expect these marks all the time."

"Perhaps we're getting a little ahead of ourselves here," Mr. MacDonald said. "Do any of the other teachers have anything to report?"

"His attitude has improved," my math teacher agreed.

"I've always loved his attitude," Ms. Carson said, "but his attendance and performance have improved."

I wasn't surprised that each teacher reported an improvement. I'd been going to class every day—or to the support room. I'd been doing homework, studying for tests, doing the readings.

If I had known that faking special education was going to be this hard, I never would have done it. But there was no choice. I had to show them that the support improved my marks. Of course, once I had the designation, I planned to start slacking off again. I didn't start this process because I wanted to work harder—it was to make my life easier.

"And finally, we need to hear from Dr. McClintock, our psychologist," Mr. MacDonald said.

This was it—the final piece. She'd tell them how badly I had done on the testing and how I was special education. I'd get the designation, get all the extra perks, and then I could slack off again. Except this time I'd have an excuse to just barely squeak by.

"I've been a psychologist for almost twenty years," she began. "I've assessed hundreds and hundreds of individuals, and I've never seen a test quite like this."

This was it. I held my breath.

"From these results I can tell you that Ed has learning disabilities."

I let out my breath. It had worked. I had fooled her. I had fooled everybody.

"In fact, from these results I can say that he has many disabilities."

I didn't need many, just one, but from the way I tanked that test I wasn't surprised.

So what? Two or three was better than none.

"It would appear that he has significant processing problems, short-, mid- and long-term-memory issues and attention deficit disorder. These results indicate that Ed is hyperactive and dyslexic, has both auditory- and visual-processing concerns, and has a very, very limited level of intelligence."

Everybody sat around the room, looking stunned.

"According to this test, it is impossible to believe that this young man could possibly function in a general school environment," she said.

"But...but he is functioning," my mother stammered.

"And doing well with our support," Miss Manning added.

"According to the results of the testing, I'm surprised Ed is able to find his way to school each morning," she said.

"But your results have to be wrong," Mr. MacDonald said.

"They are. No question," she said.

"What?" Mr. MacDonald questioned.

"They are wrong. I don't believe a thing in this test," she said, holding it up.

"But...but...what does that mean?" my father asked.

"It can only mean one thing." She paused. "Ed tried hard, very hard, to fail as badly as he possibly could."

Everybody turned and looked at me. My whole body went flush, and I felt like I was going to throw up.

"Edward?" my mother asked.

What was I supposed to say?

chapter twelve

I felt like an animal trapped in a cage.
All those eyes looking at me, questioning.
Was I supposed to admit that I'd faked the
whole thing? Should I tell them I tried to
trick them all, cost them time and money,
because I wanted to get out of doing work?
That would be insane, suicidal...It might
make me an accessory to my own murder,
as my parents might kill me.

I couldn't tell them the truth, and I'd
have to be some kind of genius to come

up with a lie good enough to explain all of this away. I was dead.

"Edward," my mother said as she reached over and placed a hand on my hand. "Is this true...did you try to fail the test?"

I shrugged. Maybe if I confessed they'd go easy on me. There was nothing else I could do. There was no alternative. I'd just tell them what I did and hope the punishment wouldn't involve being grounded for life.

"Well...I guess...maybe."

"I think I understand why he'd do that," Ellen said.

"You do?" I asked. Everybody perked up. I wanted to hear this too.

"Sometimes when people are afraid of failure they simply don't try," she said.

"That makes no sense," my father snapped.

"Really?" she asked. "You're very successful, aren't you?"

"Well..."

"I know from the family histories that you always did well in school, right through university, and you are very successful in business. You provide very well for your family."

"I try."

"You succeed. And that's what you have known. Success. Others have such little experience with success that instead of trying to win they simply don't try."

"You've seen this before?" Mr. MacDonald asked.

"I've seen many people who assume they're going to fail, so they don't try. It's very common."

"And that's what you think Edward did?" my mother asked.

"I think so, although I must admit that I've never encountered somebody who worked so hard to fail."

"Regardless," Mr. MacDonald said. "With what you're saying we can't use the test results to assess Ed's abilities. This whole assessment may not be accurate."

"The scores are practically useless," she agreed. "They don't provide any valid indication of Ed's strengths and weaknesses."

"Are you saying that we can't make a decision about Ed's status because we don't have enough information?" Mr. MacDonald questioned.

"Oh, no," Ellen said. "We do have enough information."

"We do?" I asked.

"This test was only a small part. We have interviews and conversations, the questions I asked, and most important, all of these."

She took her brief case from the floor and placed it on the table. She opened it up and removed papers...and what looked like kid's artwork...paintings and drawings and scribbling. It certainly wasn't great artwork...wait...was that my stuff?

"I asked Ed's parents to provide me with his report cards and samples of his artwork from over the years."

She passed the paintings and pictures around the table, and they went from hand to hand. I recognized some of them... these paintings were from kindergarten and grades one and two. I had no idea my mother had kept these. Obviously cars and spaceships were a pretty big focus in my life.

"Please note the vivid colors, the creative use of shape," Ellen said. "He was a very talented young man."

Some of the pictures weren't half bad— you know, for a six-year-old. This was like a little trip down memory lane.

"Please also note the name and any words. You'll see numerous reversals and numbers inserted instead of letters. Some letters are upside down, and in some cases the whole phrase is mirrored, going from right to left."

I looked at the one in my hands. It was completely backward, right to left, like I was looking at it in a mirror or it was some sort of secret spy code.

"Ed, when you write today I know that you don't do many reversals or mirrored images, but do you ever have to really think about it?"

"Mainly I think about not writing."

"But you're very good verbally," said Ellen.

"He's that for sure," Mr. Hendricks said. "Hard to get the kid to shut up in class."

"Or at home," my mother added.

"And he's very good with words, right?" asked Ellen.

"He could talk his way into or out of anything," my father agreed. "I always thought he had a great future as a salesman or a politician."

"But that level is never reflected in his writing, because writing gets in the way of his thought processes," Ellen said.

I'd never really considered it before, but she was right. I could never get the words that were racing around my head onto paper. I always had great stories that never were that great when they finally made it out. Either I couldn't spell the words I wanted, or it just took so long that I got bored and gave up.

"Ed, do you remember when you started to dislike school?"

"I've always disliked school."

"No you haven't," Ellen said. "It started in grade two."

I gave her a questioning look.

"It's all right here in black and white," she said as she held up my report cards. "In kindergarten and grade one these are the sort of comments that were used to describe you—happy and cooperative, loves learning, great attitude, a pleasure to teach." She turned to the teachers. "Does any of that sound like the Ed you see in your classes?"

"Well," Mr. Hendricks said, "when he isn't driving me crazy, I like having him around. He makes me laugh."

"A sense of humor is one of the best indications of high intelligence. You can't play with words unless you have mastery over them and the concepts they represent," Ellen said.

I thought I was in the clear, but this whole intelligence thing might lead back to me faking the test.

"But now, if we look at the comments from grade two onward..." She passed those reports around. I didn't need to look because I knew what they'd say. I didn't need to hear it again.

"In grade two everything changes. At first there are comments that Edward is having trouble with subjects. Then with each passing grade it becomes less that he is having trouble than that he is causing trouble."

I'd been in my fair share of trouble. I was on a first-name basis with the VPS since grade five.

"Edward has always been the class clown," my mother said.

"That was his way of showing everybody that he is smart, even if it meant being a smart mouth and saying things that got him in trouble." She turned to me. "You know that some of the things you say are guaranteed to get you in trouble, right?"

I nodded.

"But you still do it."

I shrugged. "Funny is funny. I can't help it if some people have no sense of humor."

"It's clear to me that Ed does have learning issues, and those issues surfaced when more emphasis was placed on written work. That's when the frustration started, and that's when he started to dislike school."

I tried to think back. I knew if anybody ever asked me I'd tell them that kindergarten or grade one were my favorite grades...was that why?

"And then what happened in school was what happened on the testing," she said. "Since you weren't having success, you decided to stop trying."

I really didn't try that hard—I knew that.

"Instead you worked hard to be seen not as a failure in school but as a success in being difficult. At some point, on some level, you decided it was better to be viewed as bad instead of stupid."

She stood up and came around the table until she was standing right beside me. She bent down until she was as close as she could get.

"Sometimes you do feel stupid, don't you?"

I'd never admitted that to anybody and certainly not in front of a dozen adults, including my parents. I felt like I was going to start crying. I nodded my head ever so slightly.

"You're not stupid," she said. "In fact, you are very, very bright."

"I'm bright?" I asked.

"Yes, bright and disabled."

"You can be both?" I asked.

"You can be," she said. "Can I ask you a question?"

I nodded.

"You don't study very much; you don't try very hard, do you?"

"Hardly at all," I said, my voice just barely a whisper.

"With a learning disability you have to try harder, study more, work longer if you want to succeed. And you can succeed."

"I've been studying a lot more. I really, really studied for that history test."

"And it showed," Mr. Hendricks said.

"I know with a combination of effort on your part and additional support that you can have great success at school," Ellen said. "And that's why I'm recommending that Ed be given a special-education designation and that he should receive appropriate support."

I felt like a gigantic weight had been lifted from my shoulders.

"But," she said and paused. "That also means that with this support everybody must demand that Ed performs at the level he's capable of. No longer should a fifty-five be considered appropriate. With the brains he has, and the support he is going to be given, we must expect no less than an eighty."

"What?" I exclaimed in shock.

"We must all demand more from him. The game playing is over. You are disabled but you are also able. No more not trying, no more feeling stupid and no more misbehaving to avoid being seen as dumb. I know you can do it. Now I have to convince just one more person."

"Who?" I asked.

She reached out and tapped me in the chest with her finger. "You."

"On that note," Mr. MacDonald said, "I am prepared to declare that Ed is exceptional, and he will start to formally receive services immediately...unless somebody has an objection?"

Nobody did.

"In that case the meeting is adjourned."

Everybody got to their feet. There was lots of friendly talking, smiling and back-slapping. My parents looked thrilled. I was really happy. There was no way this could have turned out better. For a while there, it looked like there was no way that it could end well. I'd dodged a bullet and lived to tell about it.

People started to file out of the conference room. As I went to leave there was a hand on my shoulder.

"Ed, could you wait just a minute, please," Ellen said. "I just want to have a word with you...alone."

"Sure."

Everybody exited the room, and Ellen closed the door.

"I need to ask you a question," she said. "You don't have to answer if you don't want to."

I didn't know exactly where this was going, but I had a bad feeling.

"The testing," she said. "It wasn't just that you weren't trying to pass, it's more like you were working really, really hard to fail, like you wanted to make sure we declared you special education. Did you?"

"But...but why would I do that?" I questioned, trying to sound innocent.

"You're not answering my question. Well?"

I shrugged.

"Anything you tell me will never be repeated outside this room—I'm a psychologist, and nothing that you say will be told to anybody else."

"Nothing?"

"Nothing. So?"

"Yeah, I was trying to tank it."

"But why?" she asked.

"I just thought if I was special ed, then I wouldn't have to work so hard," I admitted.

"But now you know that you really do have some learning difficulties."

"I know."

"And you also know that if you use the support and you're prepared to work harder you can succeed."

"I know."

"Then I have only one more question. Are you going to use your designation as an excuse to take it easy or as a challenge to work harder?"

I thought about how all of this started—as nothing more than an excuse to get away with doing less work. Then I thought of Elizabeth and me sitting side by side, working together in the support room.

"Ed?" she said, and I snapped out of my trance. "Well?"

Finally I thought of that forty-five out of fifty on the history test. That was what I actually could do if I tried. That did feel good.

"I'm going to work," I said. "I'm going to work hard to put the special into special education."

Author's Note

Everybody has abilities. Everybody has disabilities. Nobody is good at everything, and everybody is good at something. The secret is to accept that while we may need help in overcoming our weaknesses, that we are not defined by what we can't do, but by what we *can* do.

Eric Walters is the best-selling, award-winning author of over sixty books for juveniles and young adults. Eric lives in Mississauga, Ontario.